MICKEY AND DONALD
In The Tickle Grass

BY VINCENT JEFFERDS

A GOLDEN BOOK • NEW YORK
Western Publishing Company, Inc., Racine, Wisconsin 53404

When Mickey and Donald went to school,
They would race off when school was out,
To a special secret playing place
That no one else knew about.

The secret place they loved to go
When they rushed away from class,
They called The Laughing Meadow.
It was full of tickle grass.

It was a little hidden valley
Behind the Big Oak Wood.
No one else had found it,
And they hoped that no one would.

The first time that they went there,
They heard a laughing sound.
But even though they looked and looked,
There was no one to be found.

But they learned, when they heard it again and again,
That it wasn't a person at all.
It was simply the sound as the wind crossed the ground,
And blew through the grass three feet tall.

And each stalk of grass was even more fun
With a tickler on every end.
And if you went through the field at a run,
They would tickle both you and your friend.

But up on the hill
    lived a bitter old pill,
And the sound of
    the laughter below,
From both meadow
    and boys,
Was an infernal noise
That he felt must
    most certainly go.

So at night after dark, and with hardly a sound,
He crept quietly down the hill.
And with sickle and mower, cut the grass to the ground,
Then sneaked quietly back up the hill.

When the boys returned next day,
What they found to their dismay,
Was no laughing meadow, but instead,
Stalks of tickle grass, lying dead.

In spite of their trying,
They couldn't help crying.

Which very quickly got the attention
Of two elephants of good intention.
They both lived in the woods nearby,
And could not stand to hear kids cry.

Said Moe, "What is the matter, boys?"
His voice made a funny scratchy noise.
(You can see for yourself just how it goes,
By trying to talk while you hold your nose.)

"The mean old man cut the tickle grass,"
Said Mickey with a sob.
"It'll take at least a year to grow,
He did such a thorough job."

"We'll take care of him,"
    said Moe.
"You bet we will,"
    said his brother Joe.
"You go home to get
    some rest.
Things will turn out
    for the best."

That night they proceeded with their scheme.
They filled their trunks from the magic stream.
They ran to the laughing meadow, then
Sprayed it with water again and again.

At first nothing happened, but then, at last
The tickle grass started growing fast.

It was dawn when Moe heard his brother call,
"We can stop, the grass is three feet tall."

Up on the hill, the mean old man
Woke up chuckling about his plan.
But when he looked out his front door,
He saw the grass was as high as before.

He jumped around in such a rage,
He knocked over the parrot's cage.

He was still so angry,
He ran outside,
And kicked the old donkey
He used to ride.

"I don't know what magic could ever return it,
But with my sickle I'll cut it and burn it!"

The parrot, now free to go,
Flew down the hill to Moe and Joe,
And warned them that the mean old man
Had a new and very wicked plan.

When the mean old man
Came down that night,
They were hidden out of sight.
They hid behind a willow tree,
So they were difficult to see.

Joe grabbed the old man
with his trunk,
And gave him such
a squeeze,
That when he dropped him
to the ground,
He fell right to his knees.

He promised never again
To spoil the children's fun,
And took off up the hill
As fast as he could run.

Moe took the sickle
    and threw it so high,
You can still see it up there,
    some nights in the sky.

All of which goes to show that you can't
Win a fight with an elephant.

Next day when the boys returned to play,
The grass waved and laughed in the same old way.

Then Joe gave them a special treat.
He fixed up the mower with a seat.
Of course, the other change he made
Was to remove each cutting blade.

And nothing ever could surpass
Their rides through the waving tickle grass.